# Dear Parent:
## Your child's love of reading s

Every child learns to read in a different way and at his or her own speed. Some go back and forth between reading levels and read favorite books again and again. Others read through each level in order. You can help your young reader improve and become more confident by encouraging his or her own interests and abilities. From books your child reads with you to the first books he or she reads alone, there are I Can Read Books for every stage of reading:

### SHARED READING
Basic language, word repetition, and whimsical illustrations, ideal for sharing with your emergent reader

### BEGINNING READING
Short sentences, familiar words, and simple concepts for children eager to read on their own

### READING WITH HELP
Engaging stories, longer sentences, and language play for developing readers

### READING ALONE
Complex plots, challenging vocabulary, and high-interest topics for the independent reader

### ADVANCED READING
Short paragraphs, chapters, and exciting themes for the perfect bridge to chapter books

**I Can Read Books** have introduced children to the joy of reading since 1957. Featuring award-winning authors and illustrators and a fabulous cast of beloved characters, I Can Read Books set the standard for beginning readers.

A lifetime of discovery begins with the magical words **"I Can Read!"**

*Visit www.icanread.com for information*
*on enriching your child's reading experience.*

*For little sisters everywhere*
*—J.O'C.*

*For Xia's little sister, Fu*
*—R.P.G.*

I Can Read Book® is a trademark of HarperCollins Publishers.

Fancy Nancy: JoJo and the Big Mess
Text copyright © 2017 by Jane O'Connor
Illustrations copyright © 2017 by Robin Preiss Glasser
All rights reserved. Manufactured in China.
No part of this book may be used or reproduced in any manner whatsoever without written permission except in the case of brief
quotations embodied in critical articles and reviews. For information address HarperCollins Children's Books, a division of
HarperCollins Publishers, 195 Broadway, New York, NY 10007.
www.icanread.com

Library of Congress Control Number: 2015958385
ISBN 978-0-06-237799-9 (trade bdg.) — ISBN 978-0-06-237798-2 (pbk.)

17 18 19 20 21  SCP  10 9 8 7 6 5 4 3 2 1  ❖  First Edition

I Can Read!™

SHARED
My First READING

# JoJo
## AND THE BIG MESS

BY JANE O'CONNOR

PICTURES BASED ON THE ART OF ROBIN PREISS GLASSER

interior illustrations by Rick Whipple

HARPER
An Imprint of HarperCollinsPublishers

Hi! I am JoJo.

I make messes.

I can't help it!

Today I cook
with Nancy.
She is my big sister.

Oops!

I make a mess.

Daddy is not mad.

Into the tub I go.

Today I work
in the yard.

Oops!

I make a big mess.

Daddy is not mad.

Into the pool we go.

11

Later Freddy comes to play.

He is my pal.

We have a fight.

It is not a real fight.

It is a pillow fight.

*Ka-boom! Ka-boom!*
*Ka-boom! Ka-boom!*

Look! Look!

Feathers are flying!

We shake the pillows.
More feathers fly!

Daddy comes in.

This time he is mad.

"Clean this mess up,"
he says.

# Making a mess is fun.

Cleaning up this mess
is no fun.

At last we are done.

Freddy and I are pooped.

We plop onto the pillows.

Soon we are ready
for more fun.

I say,

"I know something fun to do."

We find paper.

We find paints.

We do not find brushes.

"That's okay," I say.

"We can use our hands."

Freddy and I paint.

Painting is fun.

It is messy.

It is pretty!

"Here. This is for you,"
I tell Daddy.

He is not mad now.

This is the best mess of all.